get red!

An Adventure in Color

Written by Tony Porto

Conceived and designed by 3CD

Tony Porto, Mitch Rice, and Glenn Deutsch

Little, Brown and Company

Boston   New York   London

3CD ♥ Mary, John, Anne; Laura, Max, Adam; Laura, Owen, and Seth

I've got this **HUGE** problem—

a whole bunch of them, really.

First of all, **EVERYONE** is mad at me.

My teacher, Mr. Fox, is **RED** hot.

Mom and Dad are even hotter (something like this).

This is **red-hot lava**—the stuff that comes out of volcanoes. Its temperature can reach over 2500°F (1371°C)!

And my goofy little brother, Rusty, likes to think he's Dad. He just looks at me like this.

To a lot of people, the color **red** means anger. This picture of Rusty is mostly yellow. Shouldn't it be mostly **red?**

See, I had a report that was due today in class. It was supposed to be about Mars, the **RED** planet.

I was going to do it, too, except you can't draw a decent picture of Mars without a **RED** crayon. And mine has **RUN AWAY!** That's my second huge problem.

How do I know my crayon has run away?

Well, that's huge problem number three. You won't believe me, but... **THE CRAYON TALKS TO ME.** It's not like I'm Doctor Dolittle or anything. Even my cat, Beans, stares off into space whenever I try to talk to her. Really, it's only this silly **RED** crayon that's talked ever since I slipped him out of his new box on the first day of class.

Hey, kid! Yeah, you . . .

In the beginning of the school year, when he was tall and proud, he'd brag about all the important RED things in the world. He talked of brave RED trucks who battled powerful RED flames without blinking a headlight.

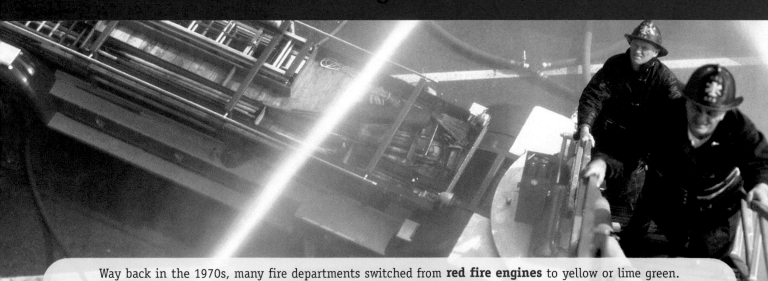

Way back in the 1970s, many fire departments switched from **red fire engines** to yellow or lime green. Nobody liked these colors much, so most have changed back to traditional **red.**

He boasted of **RED** friends who made it **BIG** in sports...

some who have appeared in every World Series since the very first one!

Every **baseball** has exactly 108 stitches holding it together. If you unraveled the **red thread** and stretched it out, it would be seven feet four inches long!

He **CROWED** about RED things on farms.

The weird **red** flesh under this rooster's beak is called a **wattle.** The **red** flesh at the top of his head is called a **comb.** Why do you think that is?

As the weeks went on, that crayon told me about so much great **RED** stuff that it started to affect my schoolwork—in good ways, at first.

In social studies, when Mr. Fox asked, "What does anyone know about Kenya, Africa?"

I raised my hand in a flash.

This is a **Samburu warrior** from Kenya. He is allowed to paint his face and hair **red** only after completing tests of manhood. By the way, he paints his chest and back **red**, too.

And in science, when we studied rain forests, I knew **TONS** of answers.

The **red-eyed tree frog** uses **red** to scare away predators. See, the frog sleeps all day. When a predator wakes it up, the frog's bright **red eyes** startle the animal, allowing just enough time to escape.

The **RED** crayon and I did projects together, too.

USE YOUR HEAD,

Traffic lights were used even before there were cars. In 1868, a lantern with **red** and green
signals was used on a London street to control horse buggy and pedestrian traffic.

During Safety Week,
we worked crayon-in-hand to make this banner.

WATCH FOR RED!

BEWARE OF DOG

An important government agency, the Occupational Safety and Health Administration (OSHA),
has designated that the color **red** means **danger.**

It was right before holiday vacation that I noticed things maybe weren't so perfect.

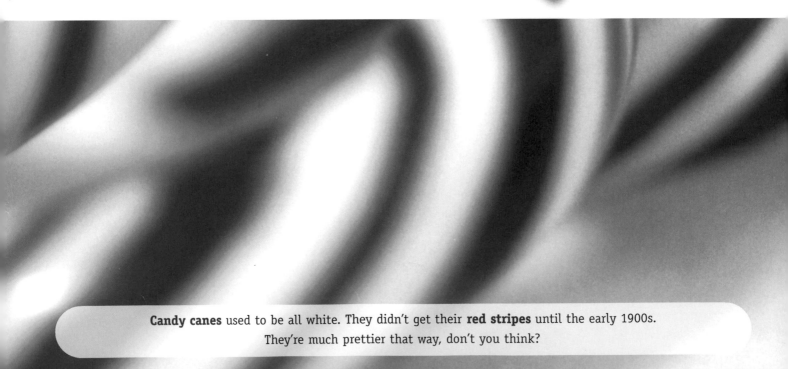

Candy canes used to be all white. They didn't get their **red stripes** until the early 1900s.
They're much prettier that way, don't you think?

First, my classmate Ruby, who thinks I'm pretty cool—or not a geek, anyway—came right up behind me in the line for recess.

She told me how she's had just about enough of me and my **MR. SMARTY-PANTS ACT** in class. And as I turned around to face her, this is the pretty sight I saw.

Because your **tongue** is **red** like a raspberry, and kind of shaped like one too, sticking your tongue out at someone is called **giving them a raspberry.**

Well, you'd think I'd be angry, but to tell the truth, all I could think about were raspberries.

And raspberries are RED...
and her tongue is VERY RED...
and, gee, I hope she isn't sick.

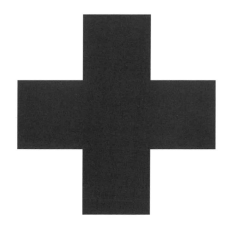

If you're really sick, you might look for this **Red Cross symbol.** It honors the country where the organization began, Switzerland. The Swiss flag has a white cross on a **red** background.

At right about that time, I also began
noticing my RED crayon "pal" was really
no pal at all. He was becoming less
and less friendly as he grew stubbier.

Once, while I was making a poster for art class, he skipped out on me. He said I wasn't gonna rub him out completely until he was good and ready.

CAN YOU BELIEVE IT!?

He left me right when I really needed him.

It took an entire day to find him, too—hiding under my Cincinnati **REDS** baseball cap.

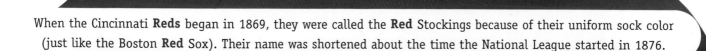

When the Cincinnati **Reds** began in 1869, they were called the **Red** Stockings because of their uniform sock color (just like the Boston **Red** Sox). Their name was shortened about the time the National League started in 1876.

As far as the art poster was concerned...

200 OF THE GREATEST RED ARTWORKS IN THE ENTIRE WORLD!

I made the best of a bad situation, and colored a **FEW** artworks less than I'd wanted.

By the way, this cool sculpture would have been on my poster if it wasn't for him.

It was supposed to be artwork number 172.

Robert Indiana is the artist who created this **red sculpture** named—you guessed it—**"Love."**
If you're ever in Philadelphia, Pennsylvania, go see it near City Hall.

Speaking of love, on Valentine's Day the **RED** stub ran off again!

This time I wasn't so lucky, 'cause you can hardly color a valentine with anything but **RED**. So I ran down to the corner store and bought these sappy cards.
That's all that was left over—really.

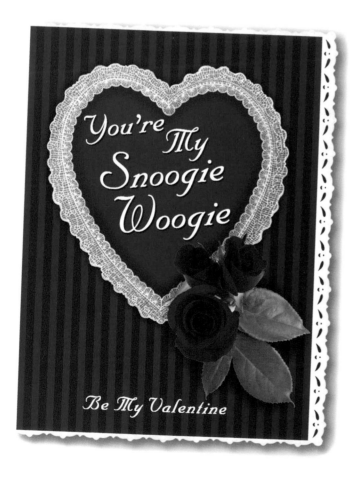

About one billion **Valentine's Day cards** are sent every year—most are **red.** Valentine's Day isn't just celebrated in the United States. Canada, Mexico, England, France, and Australia celebrate it, too.

To make matters worse, Rose at the checkout counter thought I was such a cute "Snoogie Woogie" that she just had to express herself. **YUK!**

Many brands of **red lipstick** are tinted with a dye made from ground-up, dried **insects!**

It took **THREE** days to find him after that incident. And it would have taken longer, too, if my cat Beans hadn't fished the stub out from behind Mom's tomatoes on the kitchen windowsill.

Red tomatoes are originally from America. When explorers brought them back to Europe in the 1500s, they seemed mysterious and became very popular. The French called them "apples of love."

So like I said...

I HAVE A HUGE PROBLEM!

If I don't do my Mars report, today,
Mom, Dad, and Mr. Fox are gonna blow
sky-high—not to mention the new faces
Rusty will make at me.

I've searched high and low for my crayon
"pal," and it's as if he vanished off the face
of the earth. Poof! Oh, why couldn't Mars
have been a green planet, or a blue planet,
or even a purple planet?

Hey, that's an idea...

LISTEN UP, stubby red crayon— wherever you are! I've decided to color **MARS PURPLE!**

That's right— **PURPLE!**

Purple is almost red, and it's just as good, too! In fact, Mr. fox won't notice the difference— **NO ONE WILL!**

Mars,

That was the last I saw of my RED crayon.
He was proud—too proud to pass up the Mars report.

Though he got me into some trouble,
I think I'll miss him.

the Red Planet

Uh—oh.

Hey! Hey, kid!
You were right, ya know.
PURPLE is just as good as
red. In fact, it's better.
Did you know **PURPLE** is the
color of royalty, and...

First Edition

These are some folks who helped us **Get Red:** Digital Vision, The National Geographic Society, Photodisc, Photonica, Stone, and Superstock.

Special thanks to these friends too: Jeffrey Bower, Marty Farrell, Jim Garner, Gary Gifford, Amy Hsu, Nikki Limper, Bunny Marszalek, Maria Modugno, Marko Neely, Mike Pocquat, Chuck Quinn, Mother Rice, John Sandford, Chris Sheban, Howard Yaffe, and Phil Yaffe.

Library of Congress Cataloging-in-Publication Data

Porto, Tony
    Get red! : an adventure in color/written by Tony Porto; conceived and designed by 3CD, Tony Porto, Mitch Rice, Glenn Deutsch. — 1st ed.
       p. cm.
    Summary: A boy's red crayon is very helpful at school, providing him with interesting facts about red things in the world, but as it gets stubbier with use it stops cooperating and starts hiding.
    ISBN 0-316-60940-4
    [1. Red — Fiction. 2. Crayons — Fiction. 3. Schools — Fiction.] I. Rice, Mitch. II. Deutsch, Glenn. III. Three Communication Design. IV. Title.

PZ7.P8377 Ge 2002
[E] — dc21   2001029382

10 9 8 7 6 5 4 3 2 1

TWP

Printed in Singapore

The text for this book was set in 3CD Kid Font (created by Tony Klassen) and Officina Serif.